PLANTS VS. ZOMBIES

™

OFFICIAL GUIDE TO
PROTECTING YOUR BRAINS

Written by **Simon Swatman**

Illustrated by **Adam Howling**

HARPER FESTIVAL

An Imprint of HarperCollinsPublishers

HarperFestival is an imprint of HarperCollins Publishers.

Plants vs. Zombies: Official Guide to Protecting Your Brains
Text and illustrations © 2013 by Electronic Arts Inc.
Plants vs. Zombies is a trademark of Electronic Arts Inc.
www.harpercollinschildrens.com
Library of Congress catalog card number: 2013936879
ISBN 978-0-06-222855-0
16 17 18 SCP 10 9 8
❖
Originally published by Puffin in the UK
First HarperFestival edition, 2013

DON'T LOSE YOUR HEAD

Help is (possibly) coming*

*But probably not.

Contents

Crazy Dave woz 'ere

Crazy Dave's Much, Much Better Guide to Protecting Your Brains

3. DURING THE ZOMBIE ATTACK

4. AFTERWARD

Apology

The Government would like to take this opportunity to apologize to you, the reader, for having to consult this book due to the approaching apocalyptic zombie scenario.

We seek to assure you that the undead epidemic that we, as a nation, are currently facing is entirely inherited from a previous Government and has nothing to do with us.

It's totally not our fault.

P.S. You may find it helps to refer to the zombies as "fun-dead." It just sounds a little nicer.

An Introduction from the Government

Hello, and thank you for buying this book. If you're reading it, that probably means there are zombies around (sorry about that, again) and you want to know what to do.

This publication is intended to help you—Johnny Homeowner—protect your family and home from zombie attack. Its aim is to provide valuable information about what exactly zombies are and what they want from the general public (again, that's you).

It also contains essential advice on what steps you should take to protect yourself, your family, your home and—most importantly—your brains.

THis is me, Crazy DAve

It also has anti-zombie gardening tips from me, Crazy Dave. Hi there! Just thought I should introduce myself early on, in case you were wondering why some guy had written all over your book. Wabby Wabbo!

A Quick Guide to Survival—WHOOF

If you are under zombie attack, remember to WHOOF.
Always WHOOF when zombies are around. If in doubt, WHOOF!

WHERE are the zombies?

HOW can I escape them?

ON with your shoes!

OUT of the door!

FORGIVE the zombies; it's not their fault your brains
are so delicious.

For extra safety around zombies, try adding HEN to WHOOF. It's always better to WHOOF HEN than to just WHOOF! And HEN on its own doesn't make much sense.

HOP over any zombies that are lying down.

END up somewhere safe.

NICE cup of tea on the sofa.

Look! I've been collecting these notes. The zombies keep leaving them behind. Litterbugs. :0(

Hooray! You have buried treasure in yer garden! You should dig up all those plants and get the treasure. And leave yer front door open so you can take all your treasure inside.
Sincerely, the zombies

Why Are There Zombies Outside My House?

There could be many reasons why zombies are outside your house. To be honest we just don't know at this time. *→ Pretty sure it's brains.*

However, we gave our best scientists the task of coming up with reasons why zombies might be outside your house, and this is what they came up with. You can cross them out if you know that they are wrong. It is your duty as a citizen!

- The zombies meant to go to a zoo to look at monkey brains, but got lost on the way.

- The zombies are actually real estate agents, admiring your house and wondering if you want to sell it.

- Zombies are unable to own televisions due to being undead, and they want you to tell them what's happening on their favorite shows.

- They want to use your phone to call one of their friends. It's been such a long time since they last spoke, and they feel bad about it.

- They wanted to ask for directions to the local free-range brains shop.

- Zombies are really just very friendly, and enjoy meeting new people.

- They mistook you for a pop star and just wanted to get your autograph. And maybe a quick picture?

I think this one might be about me. I do look a lot like ~~that guy~~ that guy who had that hit song in the charts that one time.

1. THE BASICS
What Is a Zombie?

In many ways zombies are like normal people but with various crucial differences: they act strange, smell awful, look like they're sick, and always want to eat your brains.

They also have the unfortunate habit of leaving parts of their bodies lying around when they drop off. You might find a leg on the lawn, or a head in the hedge, or a foot on the umm . . . sidewalk?

Not only are zombies smelly and strange, they are also very messy creatures.

DO NOT ask a zombie to pick up any body parts it has dropped. It will just shrug and try to eat your brains. Besides, garbage cans would get full very quickly if zombies kept putting their legs in them.

You should see my lawn after a zombie attack! Messy doesn't begin to describe it. Actually, come to think of it, it does.

In order for you to defeat a zombie, you must first *understand* a zombie. This does not mean being friends with a zombie (doing things like going to the movies together, taking long walks in the park, or enjoying a coffee). When zombies first appeared, our scientists tried this approach and we never saw any of them ever again.

Thankfully you have this book, so you don't have to take a zombie to the movies to get to know it, even though they do like romantic comedies and action films.

Also, I've added a bunch of stuff to this book. It was good before, but now it's BETTER.

The next section will explain what the various parts of the zombies do, so that you can either escape or defeat them.

Anatomy of a Zombie

In case you are a doctor—or you have extensive medical training —we've put together these very complicated diagrams of zombie anatomy to help you know exactly what you're up against.

Thinking part: zombies think about brains a lot (see next page).

Bad breath container: zombies have bad breath because they only eat brains. And don't brush their teeth.

Zombie guts: rumble when not full of brains. Make sloshy noises when full of brains.

Grabbing bits: avoid at all costs! Sometimes used to write notes. Grabbing bits may fall off older zombies.

Running stalks: enable zombies to chase brains, or sometimes kick a ball around in your garden. Mostly though, they're for getting brains.

A Detailed Look at the Brainial Area

Zombie writing lobe: makes the decision to write special notes about wanting to eat your brains.

Zombie chewing lobe: allows the zombie to chew brains properly. We estimate that nearly 63% of zombies have upset stomachs because they don't chew their brains properly.

Zombie conversational lobe: makes the zombie say "brains," or sometimes "braaaaaaaaaaaains" when the zombie is being overly dramatic.

A bit of a twig that got stuck in there somehow.

Spotting a Zombie

Zombies can appear at any time—you should always be on your guard. Even if you are enjoying a nice cup of tea a zombie can attack, so it's important to keep looking all around you, even while drinking tea.

This may make drinking the tea seem very difficult and even cause your neck to hurt, but this is the price we all pay for living in a zombie apocalypse.

Is that a zombie? Your action checklist:

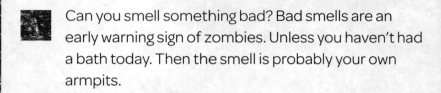

Can you smell something bad? Bad smells are an early warning sign of zombies. Unless you haven't had a bath today. Then the smell is probably your own armpits.

Can you hear a moaning sound? Zombies always make moaning sounds—they can't help it, they've got a lot to complain about. They are dead, after all.

Are the bushes moving? Zombies like to appear out of bushes and hedges and surprise you. If you see a bush moving, it is probably hiding a zombie or a really fat bird.

Can you see a zombie standing right in front of you? If you can, you probably should be running away instead of reading this checklist.

Now let us look at each of the different kinds of zombie we have so far observed.

Zombie

The most common type of zombie you will encounter. They are not particularly quick and can't defend themselves very well. Although this may make them sound like a puppy, DO NOT MISTAKE THEM FOR A PUPPY. Puppies like dog food and zombies like brains (see below).

LIKES: Brains. Any kind of brains—cold brains, hot brains, bad brains, brain salad (minus the salad).

DISLIKES: People who don't have any brains; loud music past ten o'clock at night.

Flag Zombie

When you see a Flag Zombie it means even more zombies are coming. Although he looks like a regular zombie, he's a little bit quicker*so watch out. Why is he quicker? Maybe the wind gets in the flag and pushes him along, like a ship. A zombie ship. With legs.

LIKES: Brains and flags (preferably flags with brains on them).

DISLIKES: Flags with skulls on them. They don't have any brains inside!

I eat food off the floor!

* Flag Zombies move faster than ordinary zombies and cover more ground. Two or three Peashooters work better than one.

Conehead Zombie

The Conehead Zombie wears a traffic cone on his head. He's also a zombie, which make his name *even more* suitable. Apart from looking really stylish and setting new trends in zombie headwear, the cone also protects his zombie head—making him harder to defeat than other zombies.

LIKES: Playing party games that involve cones; stopping traffic.

DISLIKES: Boring hats that aren't really tall, orange, or made of plastic.

Pole-Vaulting Zombie

Who doesn't like being out in the fresh air, getting some exercise? Not all zombies are couch potatoes—this kind of zombie likes to pole-vault. This means he can easily skip over parts of your garden in order to get to your house more quickly and eat your brains.

LIKES: Brains, especially the brains of gold medal winners.

DISLIKES: People who don't line up properly (for brains); sitting around watching TV (unless it's a program about brains).

Buckethead Zombie

The origins of the Buckethead Zombie are unclear—perhaps he was a window washer before zombification. Or maybe he just wanted to stand out from the crowd. Or maybe he forgot about the bucket entirely. Either way, the bucket makes this zombie tougher to defeat. Perhaps if you had a magnet it would be easier?

LIKES: Sunset walks.

DISLIKES: People hitting the bucket on his head. It's very loud and gives him headaches.

Newspaper Zombie

What's worse than a zombie reading a newspaper?* A zombie who is no longer reading a newspaper—because it gets him angry and he'll charge at you. Sure, you could let him keep his newspaper so he can finish the crossword, but he'll still want to eat your brains. So beware!

LIKES: Reading upside-down horoscopes.

DISLIKES: People looking over his shoulder while he reads his newspaper—that's a one-way ticket to getting-your-brains-eaten-ville.

* The newspaper is useless against plants that can lob things. It's also useless as an umbrella.

Screen Door Zombie

The Screen Door Zombie liked the last house he visited so much, he kept the screen door! And ate the homeowner's brains, obviously. The door protects this zombie from certain things, but not everything. Our scientists tried throwing breadcrumbs at him but that didn't work—he just ended up looking like a big chicken finger.

LIKES: Eating brains through a screen door (he thinks it makes him look sophisticated).

DISLIKES: Glass or wooden doors—it's impossible to eat anything through them unless they've got a mail slot and eating brains through a mail slot just looks silly.

Football Zombie

This zombie appears to be a football fan. Our scientists first encountered the Football Zombie at night, and his helmet and padding make him tougher to defeat. But once the padding is gone he's just like any other zombie. Just make sure he doesn't get a "touchdown" on your brains.

LIKES: Playing hard, and eating brains hard (we're not sure how you eat brains hard—perhaps you do it in the dark).

DISLIKES: People who don't give 110% (of their brains).

The helmet is metal, so try a Magnet-shroom. I once saw a hedgehog!

Dancing Zombie

Just like the rest of us did in the carefree days before the apocalypse, this zombie likes to dance. Unfortunately for us, when you see a Dancing Zombie it means he'll have four backup dancers not far behind him. Zombies aren't really ones to dance alone. They get very self-conscious and feel embarrassed.

LIKES: Dancing. Favorite moves include the brain-bump, freestyle brain-dancing, and the tango.

DISLIKES: Anyone who says disco is dead. Disco is *un*dead.

Backup Dancer Zombie

Backup Dancer Zombies tend to surround the Dancing Zombie. They'll probably cheer the Dancing Zombie on as well, if you leave them long enough—though our scientists advise against this (what with zombies eating your brains, etc.).

LIKES: Dancing the gray matter cha-cha-cha.

DISLIKES: People calling them backup dancers. They're *background artistes*.

Remember— backup dancers work as a team. Stop one, and the rest stop too!

I once stopped sleeping for a whole day!

Ducky Tube Zombie

If your garden has a pool, there's a good chance you'll see a Ducky Tube Zombie. Sometimes a few of them will appear at once from under the water. Our scientists advise against challenging them to a game of water polo or who can hold their breath the longest (the zombies always win that one because they are dead and don't need to breathe).

LIKES: Being wet.

DISLIKES: Towels.

Snorkel Zombie

Snorkel is a funny word! Thrrrrrrrp.

The Snorkel Zombie is another pool pest that our scientists have observed.* Because they have a snorkel, they can move underneath the water in a pool, so they have an annoying habit of sneaking up on you. More observant readers may ask, "Why does a zombie have a snorkel, they don't need air?" Our scientists have concluded that this zombie just likes biting things.

LIKES: Aqua-brains.

DISLIKES: Aqua-lungs.

* Yeah, well, I observed that Snorkel Zombies can be hit by catapult plants and dragged down by Tangle Kelp.

Mullet Zombie

For some zombies, eating brains is just not enough in life. Some, like Mullet Zombie, ask much bigger questions than "Braaaaaaaaaaaaains?" Mullet Zombie asks, "Should my hair be long or should it be short?"

Sadly, he could never choose, and so decided instead to go with a mullet. Sure, his hair might look funny—but it'll be the last laugh you'll ever have when he's eating your brains.

LIKES: Anything denim; fingerless leather gloves; loud rock music.

DISLIKES: People who can actually choose a haircut.*

* Hey, just wear a saucepan over your head like me. Then it doesn't matter what haircut you have BECAUSE THE SAUCEPAN NEVER COMES OFF!

Zombie Bobsled Team

If you spot an ice trail, then there's a good chance the Zombie Bobsled Team won't be far behind. Our scientists found that melting the ice can stop the bobsled team, though not by pouring hot water on the trail—it takes too long to boil the kettle each time.

LIKES: Iced brains.

DISLIKES: Brain soup.

BRAINS OR BUST

Remember, there's no "I" in team, but there is in brains! I think. How do you spell things?

Dolphin Rider Zombie

What could be more delightful in the middle of a zombie apocalypse than a dolphin? The gentle, relaxing call of this majestic creature soothes your ears and nerves. Well unfortunately the dolphin is also a zombie. Sorry.

Dolphin Rider Zombie is similar to the Pole-Vaulting Zombie, except that in this case the pole is a dolphin, and it can sing. And it isn't made of wood. And it shoots water out of a blowhole above its face. Apart from that they're identical.

LIKES: Bottlenoses.

DISLIKES: People who are at "cross porpoises" with him. Ha ha. That's just a little Government joke.*

*Someone told me a joke once. It was hilarious.

Jack-in-the-Box Zombie

Don't be fooled—the Jack-in-the-Box Zombie is not going to give you a present, even if it's your birthday. The box*explodes, which is good if he's around other zombies but not so good if he's lining up for a hot dog at a fairground. There'd be mustard and buns everywhere.

LIKES: Jack-in-the-boxes, especially if they include Jack's brain.

DISLIKES: Empty boxes.

* The jack-in-the-box is metal though, so you can take it away with a trusty Magnet-shroom....

Balloon Zombie

It's not just hedges and swimming pools that zombies can pop out of. Our scientists have observed this zombie floating around tied to a balloon, making him harder to defeat.* How did he get the balloon? Perhaps he was at a Halloween party, and won it for having the best costume (a zombie).

LIKES: The air up there.

DISLIKES: The brains down there (he can't reach them).

* Not so tough if you have a Cactus or a Cattail. They can pop balloons.

Wooo-haaa!

Digger Zombie

So far we've educated you on zombies that come at you (most of them) and zombies that are above you (see previous page). Now we'd like to make you aware of the zombie that digs tunnels under your lawn and pops out near your house. He's basically like a big mole, apart from the fact that he waves a pickax around and wants to eat your brains. So nothing like a mole, really.

LIKES: Getting his jeans dirty.

DISLIKES: Not having any soil to dig through. He just gets bored when that happens.

Magnet-shroom, Gloom-shroom, Starfruit, and Split Pea will do the job here.

Pogo Zombie

The Pogo Zombie uses his stick to jump all over your garden. He makes a nasty mess of your lawn and plants, and also makes a really annoying sound.

Sproing! Sproing! Sproing! Sproing! Sproing! Sproing! Sproing! Sproing! Sproing! Sproing! Sproing! Sproing! Sproing! Sproing! See what we mean? If you've found this paragraph annoying to read, imagine what it's like to *hear* him jump around all over the place. *Sproing! Sproing! Sproing!* You get the idea.*

LIKES: Going *sproing! Sproing! Sproing!*

DISLIKES: Not going *sproing! Sproing! Sproing!*

* Stop the sproinging
with a Tall-nut!
Please. Do it for
me. Sproing.

Zombie Yeti

As far as we know, nobody has ever actually encountered the Zombie Yeti, but he is believed to be a tough zombie to defeat. Our scientists say he probably has to be, what with being all hairy and coming from the Himalayan Mountains. Zombie Yeti is a rare and curious creature. Curious about the taste of your brains, that is.

LIKES: Yodeling (he grew up in the mountains after all).

DISLIKES: Being called the zombie Abominable Snowman. Snowmen have carrots for noses. Does he look like he has a carrot for a nose?

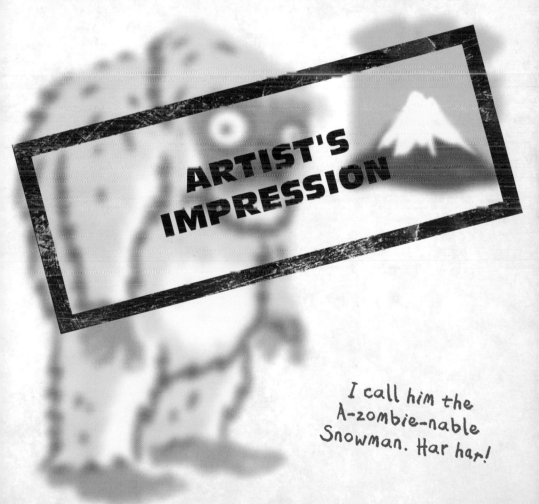

ARTIST'S IMPRESSION

I call him the A-zombie-nable Snowman. Har har!

Bungee Zombie

Like the Balloon Zombie, the Bungee Zombie attacks you from above. He uses a bungee rope to drop down and either steal things from your garden or drop other zombies onto the lawn. Before he appears, you may see a target and hear a "YEEEE-HAH!"—although our scientists have noted that this is also true of overly enthusiastic cowboys. *

LIKES: Living life to the fullest (well, the afterlife at least).

DISLIKES: People who snap rubber bands. That's just cruel.

* I want to be a ~~Ninja~~ ~~cowboy~~ ~~spaceman~~ tennis player.

Ladder Zombie

We can only speculate what the Ladder Zombie used to be before he turned zombie. Did he clean windows for a living? Or cut hedges? Or was he just trying to get a good view of an exciting sports event? What our scientists tell us now is that he uses the ladder as a shield, as well as for climbing over any obstacles you put in his way. If only he'd just clean the windows of your house, instead of trying to eat your brains through them.

LIKES: Ladder martial arts. Rung-fu?

DISLIKES: Magnets, people who don't say sorry when they sneeze.

Bad news. Snow peas and flaming peas can't hurt ladder. That's one tuffough ladder. Who'd have thunked it?

Catapult Zombie

Like the members of the Zombie Bobsled Team, this is another zombie that can drive. How he got a driver's licence is beyond us. It makes a cruel mockery of the road laws of our green and pleasant land, not to mention basic health and safety.

So far, our scientists have also been unable to determine why he fires basketballs from his vehicle—perhaps he knows someone who runs a sports shop and can get them at a discount?

LIKES: Slam dunks; brain rebounds.

DISLIKES: Running out of basketballs.

I love basketball.
Especially when they
get a hole-in-one.
Fore!

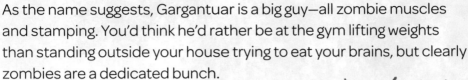

As the name suggests, Gargantuar is a big guy—all zombie muscles and stamping. You'd think he'd rather be at the gym lifting weights than standing outside your house trying to eat your brains, but clearly zombies are a dedicated bunch.

No pain, no brain! Wabbo.

He is normally seen kindly giving a piggyback ride to a tiny zombie passenger called Imp, who he will throw at your house (which is less kind of him). Imp may be small, but don't underestimate him.

LIKES: Stamping on things; playing the ukulele.

DISLIKES: People who can't look past his bulging undead muscles and see the sensitive zombie within.

Want to take out Gargantuar with one hit?

Try Lawn Mowers, Pool Cleaners, or Roof Cleaners! Not so tough NOW are we, Mr. Big Stampy Feet?

Dr. Zomboss

Meet Dr. Edgar George Zomboss, the zombie who seems to be in charge of all the zombies. With a pleasant-sounding name like Edgar, you'd have thought he would be quite receptive when the Government asked to meet with him and discuss all this "zombie apocalypse business" over a nice pot of tea. But no, he wasn't having any of it.

Dr. Zomboss likes to get around in the Zombot, a giant robot that fires ice and fireballs when it bends down (our scientists have a theory that this is when it's at its weakest).

LIKES: The in-depth discussion of dead things; world domination.

DISLIKES: Not dominating the world.

Other Possible Sightings

Trash Can Zombie

Sadly the Trash Can Zombie isn't here to pick up litter, or to offer helpful tips on how to recycle your vegetable peelings or glass. If you've been closely studying this book you will have realized by now that this zombie wants to eat your brains. He just uses the trash can to protect himself, not tidy up. What a shame.

That said, Trash Can Zombie is all about recycling waste. In this case he's eager for you to recycle the "waste" brains sloshing about in your skull into something better—his dinner.

Target Zombie

Target Zombie holds up a big bull's-eye target as a defense. Ha! The joke's on him; he's basically a walking target. Or a shuffling target, at least.

Peashooter Zombie

A rare sort, Peashooter Zombie has a Peashooter for a head and fires peas. This is why our scientists have called him Peashooter Zombie. They're very clever people you know.

Now, you might enjoy peas with your dinner, but when you combine a pea and a zombie you're in for big trouble. Big green trouble. That fires peas. Dinner doesn't sound so appealing now, eh?

Wall-nut Zombie

Wall-nut Zombie has a Wall-nut for a head. He's a tough fellow to crack! Get it? Wall-nut? Crack? Who says people who write zombie survival guides for the Government don't have a sense of humour!

OK, I get it Mister Government book—writing guy!

Being half nut, Wall-nut Zombie knows how to easily crack a tough shell and get to the nut inside. And by shell we mean your skull. And by nut we mean your brains. Sorry about that.

Gatling Pea Zombie

Another rare-but-dangerous zombie. Gatling Pea Zombie fires four peas at a time. If only he wasn't trying to eat your brains he would be quite handy to have around. Especially if you wanted some peas to go with your chicken fingers.

Or tacos. Pea tacos are a thing, right?

Tall-nut Zombie

Because he has a giant nut for a head, Tall-nut Zombie takes a lot of damage before you can defeat him. Just be careful not to spend too long laughing at him, or calling him names like "nut face," "shell features," or "the lanky dead."

Jalapeño Zombie

Jalapeño Zombie has a chili pepper for a head. While he may be good for spicing up food, he also has the tendency to explode all over your lawn. It's a sad fact of the zombie apocalypse—food will be significantly blander and less spicy. But at least you're still alive (for now).

I can still get meat sticks though, right? RIGHT?

Squash Zombie

Another unpleasant vegetable-zombie hybrid, Squash Zombie shouldn't be confused with the sport of squash. At least if he were playing a sport he wouldn't be trying to eat your brains.

Giga-Football Zombie

One of those football types, thankfully he's a very rare specimen. Our scientists note that he's fast and tough—and possibly says things like "hut hut hut" as he runs around.

I slept in a hut once.

Giga-Gargantuar Zombie

After months of careful observation and dozens of scientists getting their brains eaten, we conclude that this zombie is <u>one of the toughest out there</u> ("there" in this case meaning your garden). You can spot him by his glowing red eyes. Maybe he's been crying over all those scientists who got their brains eaten? Or perhaps he suffers from hay fever.

HAY!

Catapult Baseball Zombie

This rare specimen lobs basketballs during any baseball games you play. Does anyone else find this confusing?

I'm never confused. Except for sometimes when anything happens.

Baseball Zombie

Not much is known about this zombie, but we can say for certain that his baseball cap has a picture of a brain on it and he wears the cap the right way. What a sensible guy he is.

You say that, government type people—but Lawn Mowers, Pool Cleaners, and Roof Cleaners can beat them instantly. Hooray!

BASEBALL ZOMBIE

The Undead Through the Ages

Sadly, zombies are not a new menace. They have been active throughout history. For educational purposes, your Government has provided this handy timeline highlighting important events in zombie-related history. Please study it carefully!

Dawn of Time

Humans with brains exist.

431 BC

The catapult is invented by Greek engineers. Zombies steal it and use it to launch themselves over high walls to get to the Greek engineers' brains behind them.

30 Minutes After Dawn of Time

Zombies with an appetite for human brains exist.

180 BC

Deadus Zombius becomes leader of the Roman Empire, after winning a decisive victory by eating the brains of his rivals. This technique is repeated by politicians throughout the ages, though they won't ever admit it.

12 AD

A zombie chips his tooth after trying to bite the head off a statue of the Egyptian queen Cleopatra. Another zombie trips over a mummy's bandages, making this the clumsiest period in zombie history.

492

Pope Gelasius is chased around a cathedral by zombies who want to eat his brains. He only escapes after hiding in a cupboard for a week and waiting until the zombies get bored and leave.

What's wrong with living in a cupboard?

213

Famous Greek mathematician Brainius celebrates his 18th birthday. Zombies gatecrash the party and enjoy a special birthday feast at his expense.

553

The first recorded instance of someone asking, "Why did the zombie cross the road?" After crossing the road, the zombie then eats their brains—thus ensuring no one tries to turn this into a joke until at least 1968.

843

A zombie is accidentally crowned king of Germany when he tries on the crown in a moment of boredom. The subsequent feast is cut short when the new king eats everyone's brains.

701

The first known song is performed by a zombie, after the zombie stubs his toe on a rock. The song —called "Braaaaaaaaiiins OUCH! Braaaaaaaaiiins"— spends the next sixteen weeks on the charts.

1066

William the Conqueror, Duke of Normandy, invades England. Within ten minutes of landing on the beach at Hastings, his brains are eaten by zombies. In the traditional British seaside style, they enjoy it with chips and lots of salt and vinegar.

921

The Vikings invade England, only to retreat back home a day later (minus their brains). The remaining Vikings (with brains) decide it's a really good idea to wear big metal helmets at all times in the future.

1278

The first recorded instance of a zombie riding a horse. Minutes after learning to ride, the zombie bangs his head on a tree branch and falls off, thus continuing the rich tradition of zombie clumsiness.

I guess they hadn't invented saucepans yet?

1687

Zombies decide that saying "urrrrrrrrrrrrrrrr" is almost the same as saying "arrrrrrrrrrrrrrrr," so they decide to become pirates. That, and the fact that they really like the hats. Plus some of them are already missing limbs, so the whole wooden leg thing is really convenient.

This bit is **definitely** true. I saw Pirate Zombies when I went **back in time**. Have I mentioned I can do that?

Oh yeah, I mentioned it on page 122. This **proves** I can time travel, because it's on a page in the future!

1688

Zombie pirates discover they get really, really seasick, so decide to stop being pirates and stick to dry land.

1835

A shoot-out between two cowboy zombies lasts over three weeks because they are dead and getting shot doesn't make one bit of difference. The shoot-out only ends when the townspeople complain about all the noise and demand an end so they can get a good night's sleep.

1921

Tension between humans and the undead briefly ceases after zombies get jobs in a toy factory testing whoopee cushions.

2014

Some crackpots are saying that zombies are going to take over the world any day now, but your Government would like to assure you that this is not going to happen.

Take a look out the window Mister Governments! And then come and buy some stuff from me.

What Do the Zombies Want?

Now that this manual has established how to spot the zombies, and has wildly speculated on where they came from, it's time to explore what the zombies might want from us.

Most of us reading this book have brains, and, through careful observation of our scientists getting their brains eaten, we have been able to establish that this is clearly the main thing the zombies want.

However—zombies have also been observed eating plants. Why might this be?

i) They enjoy a balanced diet and like a fresh and healthy side salad to go with their brains.

ii) Zombies are easily confused and think that brains grow on trees—or, more precisely, on the ground.

iii) Eating plants is just practice for eating brains.

iv) Boredom. Don't pretend you've never nibbled on some grass or a leaf when you've been bored.

I once ate a plank of wood. Tummy hurt afterward.

To work out exactly what zombies want from us, we have compiled the following list of what zombies definitely *DON'T* want from us, in an attempt to narrow down the list of possible zombie demands.

i) They don't want a ride in your car. Zombies are fine with walking/shuffling everywhere.*

ii) They don't want to see your vacation pictures. Zombies have no interest in your travel experiences.

iii) They don't want to talk about the weather. Zombies want to eat brains come rain or shine.

iv) They don't want to trade recipes. Unless it's for things like gray matter stew, cranium cake, or brain-stem surprise. MEAT STICKS?

v) They don't care to hear where you bought your clothes from. Unless you're wearing a hat, then they might ask to "see it"—this is usually followed by some brain eating.

* My car is too full of seeds and other garden stuff to give zombies a lift.

Zombie Myths

It has come to our attention that various myths are circulating among the population about zombies. This is potentially dangerous, so we will now attempt to clear up these untruths once and for all.

 Zombies are great at conversation.
This is simply not true. Zombies talk about nothing other than brains—and even then, conversation is limited to just saying the word "brains" and nodding.

 Zombies will shrivel up if they touch salt.
This is only true of slug zombies.

*I have **never** seen a slug zombie. These guys don't know what they're talking about! Wabby.*

 Zombies are party animals.
Scientific research has proven conclusively that zombies are in no way "party animals." They usually like to be tucked up in bed with a good book by around ten o'clock at night. *I do not think so.*

Zombies are good at making cakes.
While zombies are good at mixing up eggs and flour (they enjoy repetitive tasks), they are terrible at remembering to turn the oven on, or remembering to set the timer. Or remembering anything, basically.

A zombie's favorite color is blue.
Everyone likes blue, right? Not zombies. They like pink. *Brain pink.*

Zombies are made of cheese.
This is simply ridiculous. Have you ever tried to eat some zombie on a cracker? It tastes horrible—like blue cheese, only stinkier.

CHEESE

Dead vs. Undead: Crucial Differences

As stated before, in many ways zombies are very similar to us non-zombies: walking around, making noises with our mouths, etc.

But it would be foolish to think that *all* dead things are zombies. There are some crucial differences between the dead and the undead, and we hope that this handy chart will help you understand.

Understand? Is **cheese** dead?

DEAD	UNDEAD
Generally very still, except for during an earthquake or next to some very loud music.	Typically walks slowly, except when taking part in a sport.
Has no appetite for anything.	Eats brains (and sometimes plants).
Usually found in a graveyard.	Usually found in your garden or house.
Almost never wears a hat.	Looks good in a variety of hats
Impossible to have a conversation with.	Limited conversational opportunity (brains, eating brains, the best place to get fresh brains, etc.).
Likes to be alone.	Very social, enjoys mixing in the zombie horde.
Sometimes visited by relatives to pay their respects.	Prompts relatives (and everyone else, for that matter) to run off screaming in all directions.

2. PROTECTING YOURSELF AND YOUR HOME (AND YOUR BRAINS)

There's an old saying that goes, "A man's home is his castle." If only this were true and we were all living in castles. That would mean every homeowner could simply pull up the drawbridge and watch with merry delight as zombies tumbled into the moat. Having said that, a moat full of zombies would probably drive down property prices in the area.

To stand a chance in the zombie apocalypse, we suggest you choose a room in your home to be your ZITS (Zombie Incident Total Safety) room. At the first sign of a zombie outbreak, proceed to ZITS!

Having a big pile of tires in your garden also does this! Or at least that's what the letter said.

Choosing ZITS

i) Smell

The ZITS room should not only keep zombies out physically, but should also block out their smell. Zombies smell awful, as they don't take showers or bathe. They don't even use deodorant (apart from *Old Spicy Brains*).

ii) Noise

Zombies also make an awful lot of noise. This can be very annoying if you're trying to sleep or play a fun game like charades. Nothing makes charades more difficult than having dozens of moaning zombies on the other side of your door. Make your ZITS as soundproof as possible. Failing that, stuff cotton wool in your ears.

iii) Privacy

Improve your ZITS by blocking out the window. You can either put sandbags against the glass or paint it black. Or you could just close the curtains. If you don't, you'll have to deal with a zombie horde staring into your living room. Zombies are a very nosey bunch and have very poor manners.

iv) Alternatively . . .

If none of this is possible, or you find yourself outside during a zombie attack, simply lie facedown on the ground with your fingers in your ears. This way you can neither see nor hear the zombies. For extra safety, we recommend loudly humming the national anthem.

Hey there! It's us—yer new neighbors.
We made too many **brownies** and we would like to give you some. If you **clear the garden** for us we can come over and you can eat **brownies** and we can eat brains maybe?

Sincerely, yer ~~zom~~ neighbors

Home Defense

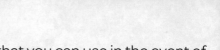

There are many items around the home that you can use in the event of a zombie attack. In the following pages we will describe how you may use these common household items to defend yourself from the undead.

Library of books

A large collection of books is an invaluable resource, providing handy facts and information on the world around you, as well as countless hours of literary entertainment. Books can also be thrown at zombies if they invade your home. Because of this, we recommend a sturdy set of encyclopedias. Quickly read the book before you throw it, and you can educate yourself while defending against zombies.

Dining table

Perfect for eating a traditional family meal on—or for hiding under, if the traditional family meal happens to be interrupted by zombies eager to feast on your gray matter.

Big hats

Remember, saucepans also make good hats.

Big hats are perfect for keeping the sun out of your eyes and off your head on sweltering summer days. They are also a great way of confusing a zombie. Simply throw one over his face and he'll think it's nighttime. He'll then become deeply fashion conscious and find the nearest mirror in order to make sure the hat looks good on him.

Chairs

Not only can you sit on a chair, but you can also stand on it: perfect for avoiding any zombies that have infiltrated your home and are under thirteen inches tall. Granted, this may be a rare occurrence, but it can't be ruled out.

I think it can, Government guys.

A rubber ball

Consider bouncing a brightly colored rubber ball off the walls in your home. Although we are unable to test this theory, our scientists are convinced that nobody—even the undead—is able to resist the charm and fun of a bouncy rubber ball.

Dirty laundry

Chances are, the zombie apocalypse means your washing machine no longer works. Dirty laundry is piling up everywhere—and, as with our scientists' theory about rubber balls, we predict that even zombies will not enjoy being near your stinking clothes. Wear as many filthy layers as possible and stay very still. Hopefully they will confuse you with a pile of last week's underwear.

Treadmills

The more health-conscious among you may have a treadmill in the home. This is an ideal zombie deterrent. Simply put it outside the door and the zombie will not be able to get in. Make sure the treadmill is going *against* the direction of your home—otherwise you'll just be helping the zombie to eat your brains more quickly.

Lawn mowers are better.

IN CASE OF FIRE

Always have i) a bucket of water and ii) a bucket of sand close at hand in case of fire. If there is no fire, declare that day "a vacation" and use the sand and water to pretend you are on an exotic beach somewhere. Write imaginary postcards to friends and pretend you have a suntan.

Emergency Supplies

Prepare your ZITS for a stay of at least one week. Our scientists calculate that after that time you and your family will become incredibly bored and would probably welcome having your brains eaten by a zombie. Your Government recommends that you have the following items handy:

Carrots: in case you need to befriend a horse.

A portrait of Her Majesty the Queen: as a reminder that even the queen must prepare for a zombie attack.

A clock: to spend hours staring at and to know when it is the appropriate time to eat.

Sack of lentils: not for eating (hopefully things will never get that bad), but for playing fun games to pass the time. We suggest such amusing games as "Find the Lentil," "Musical Lentils," and "How Many Lentils Can I Get in My Pockets?"

A towel: see first-aid tips on the next page.

Bananas: it's essential to keep up a healthy diet during any undead rampage, so be sure to eat plenty of fresh fruit and vegetables. Bananas are high in potassium, and the skins can be used to slip up any attacking zombies (or your friends and family, in case you need to lighten the mood with a practical joke).

Pen and paper: useful for keeping a diary, or drawing pictures of a dog riding a bicycle. Trust us, you'll have plenty of free time to draw pictures of a dog riding a bicycle.

This list make no mention of beards. This is a grave mistake.

First Aid

The ability to perform first aid is an invaluable skill during a zombie apocalypse. Unless you happen to be (or know) a doctor, you should memorize the following steps to help treat a wide variety of wounds.

**You will need:
a towel.**

Two towels, to be on the safe side.

If you have been injured in a non-zombie-related incident:

i) Wrap a towel around the wound.

ii) Wait until you get better.

iii) Relax.

If you have been injured in a zombie-related incident:

i) Wrap a towel around the wound.

ii) Ask any other persons to leave your home and lock the door.

iii) Relax.

Crazy Dave's Much, Much Better Guide to Protecting Your Brains

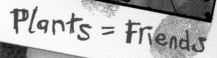

Plants = Friends

Intro

Greetings neighbor! First off, let me say  hi to you. Hi! I call myself Crazy Dave (although some people prefer to say I'm just eccentric). In many ways, I'm just like you: I laugh, I cry, I appreciate a good sunset—sometimes I eat food off the floor.

This is me, Crazy Dave

Like you never eat food off the floor!

I have no idea who took this photo

Second off, you're probably asking questions like "Why is this book inside my government handbook" or "Who wrote all over my book?"

70

Well, it's like this. I think this book's pretty good, but it doesn't have much about plants (I love plants) or other important stuff like tacos and beards. So I've made up for that by adding some great extra info!

look at Wall-nut's little face!

I'm pretty much the fountain of all knowledge when it comes to plant stuff. Wait, is fountain the right word? ✖Sheesh! I've only just started writing this book and already you're putting pressure on me to do words right. ✖✚☺〰

Anyway, I hope these words help you out in your fight against zombies.

You're welcome!

Super-Gigantic List of Handy Things to Have

OK, so there are zombies. What are you gonna do now? Well, you need stuff otherwise you won't be doing much except getting your brains ~~are~~ munchy-munched. None of us want that to happen, so I've made this **MASSIVE** list of handy things to have.

※ **Notebook and pencil**—so you can keep track of how many zombies are around. And so you can draw pictures of bacon.

※ **Saucepans**—for cooking dinner (bacon), or for wearing on your head (this helps keep rain off and also protects those brains).

※ **Sunglasses**— I am one pretty cool guy. Always be cool, like me.

Favorite headwear

72

* Washing up gloves—for removing bits of zombies you find in your house. And also for washing up dishes. Hey, I'm "Crazy Dave," not "Tons of Dirty Plates Dave."

* Belt—to keep trousers up. One time I left the house and my trousers kept falling down because I forgot to wear a belt. Just imagine having to pull your trousers up while being attacked by zombies! So now you understand why I added a belt to this list.

* Bacon—because bacon.

* Extra bacon—just in case. I'm always prepared like that.

* Hidden supply of "backup bacon." I call this BACKCON. Pretty clever huh?

This list isn't nearly as gigantic as I thought it would be.

CRAZY DAVE'S BONUS TIP

Always remember where you put your car keys. I can't. Maybe you can help?

Plants and Their Uses

I'm a pretty enthusiastic garden-type-guy and one thing I've noticed is plants help you defeat zombies. You think plants are just pretty and green? ~~M~~ No, they're real good at getting rid of zombies.

But ~~MOST~~ beating up on zombies (I'll talk about this in a while) is just one thing plants can do. They're also good for a bunch of other stuff.

Some plants (like **tomato** plants or **lettuce** plants) go with bacon. They make bacon taste even better. One time, at school, there was a teacher who was always telling me that eating so much meat is unhealthy. But since then that teacher has had her brains eaten by a big **zombie**. So who's the unhealthy one **now**, Mrs. Teacher Lady? At least I still have **brains** in my head.

Some plants look nice. People have them on their lawn so they can have long talks with neighbors about them. They say things like "I like that so-and-so bush you have, neighbor."

I also put things on my lawn so I can have long talks with neighbor-people. For example, once I put a **big** pile of car tires on my lawn. I thought neighbors would say "Hey neighbor, I **really** like that huge pile of tires on your lawn. Do you like cars? **Cars** are pretty awesome."

But no, neighbors never said that. They just asked me to **get rid** of the tires and then never talked to me again. People are **weird** like that, which is why I like **plants** so much.

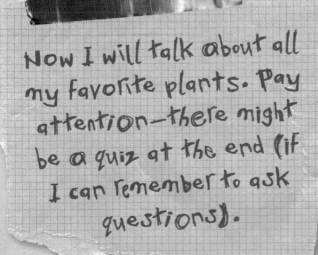

Now I will talk about all my favorite plants. Pay attention—there might be a quiz at the end (if I can remember to ask questions).

75

Peashooter

Peashooters shoot peas. If they shot shoes, then they'd be called shoe shooters. But they don't so they aren't— will I have to explain all the obvious stuff like this to you? Peashooters are your go-to plant when stopping zombies. They grow quick and shoot peas real fast.

Sunflower

Sunflowers don't shoot anything at zombies, but they do make lots of sun, which will help your other plants grow big and strong. Sun is the plant version of meat.

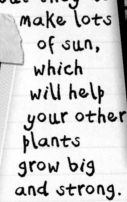

Trust me on this one.

Cherry Bomb

Cherry Bombs look all sweet and nice, but they can ~~smell~~ **blow UP** zombies. They have a short fuse, so they explode almost straight after you plant them. Some say I have a short fuse, but if your supermarket said they don't sell saucepan hats you'd have knocked those cans of beans over as well.

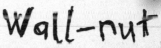

Wall-nut

Wall-nuts help defend your plants from zombies (unless they are jumpy zombies). Wall-nut is a deep thinker and difficult to get inside of— I tried once, and I hurt my teeth. I thought about trying to hit one with a saucepan, but then I remembered that I freak out if my saucepan isn't on my noggin at all times.

Potato Mine

Potato Mines will **explode** when those stupid zombies tread on them, but they can take a while to arm themselves, so I suggest you plant them before the zombies get right in your face.

The worst thing about a zombie in your face is the smell. They got some toilet-breath, those zombies.

Snow Pea

The Snow Pea slows zombies down by **freezing** them. Turns them into a big zombie ice pop! One time it was a really hot day and I had an ice pop. Since the zombie apocalypse my freezer doesn't work and everything **melts**. It makes me sad when lovely ice pop juice drips everywhere.

But it still tastes nice when I lick it off the floor.

Repeater

The Repeater fires peas **twice as fast** as Peashooter, so he's real good at keeping zombies away. Sometimes I think Repeater keeps everyone away because he's scared of showing the real him. Repeater just wants to be loved.

Chomper

Chompers can **eat** a zombie whole. **Yeah!** How d'you like getting chewed up, zombies? Problem with Chomper is that he takes ages to chew his meals, so while he's finishing up he can get **attacked**. It's important to chew food properly though.

I once ate a whole loaf of bread without chewing and immediately regretted it.

Puff-shroom

Puff-shroom may not have a big range, but mushrooms grow well at night (they sleep during the day, just like my no-good cousin Ralph. He's so **lazy**). Sometimes the zombies attack at night—maybe they get **bored** or there is no good TV to watch. How am I supposed to know?

I'm a gardener, not an expert on zombie social life.

Sun-shroom

Sun-shroom gives your plants **sunshine**, which is good when there is no sun, like at night. Or **Thursdays.**
I guess he gives away all that sunshine because he hates it. Sounds like a ▓▓ **nightmare** to go on vacation with, right?

Fume-shroom

This guy puts out a bad fume, which is good news because the **stink** can go through screen doors, ladders, and other #*# things zombies defend themselves with. Not so clever now are we, **Mr. Zombie?** Standing on my lawn. Holding a **door.** Getting **mushroom** smells on you.

Whoops, I tripped.

Hallo, this iz the zombies.
One of us dropped hiz **keys** in yer garden and now he can't get into hiz house. Pleaz can you get rid of all your **plants** so we can look for the keys?
Thanks, buddy!

Sincerely, **the zombies**

Hello,
we are collecting canned goods for charity. Is it OK if we come into your house and haul them away? Pleeze let us into yer houze.

It's for a really good cause.

Sincerely, the zombies

Hypno-shroom

The Hypno-shroom makes zombies turn around and **attack** other zombies. He only has a single use, but Hypno-shroom is one pretty persMuasive guy. I wonder how well Hypno-shroom would do if he ran for **President** of the USA?

Scaredy-shroom

This one's good for early defense but, as his name suggests, he gets **scared** and hides when zombies get too close. Can you blame him? Zombies ~~I~~ **are not nice** and I would get scared too if it wasn't for the fact that I have a ~~special~~ **saucepan** hat to protect my brain-parts.

Ice-shroom

When you plant the Ice-shroom it **freezes** all the zombies for five and a half seconds. Pretty **cool** huh? I don't understand why Ice-shroom looks so ~~~~ **grumpy** all the time—maybe it's because he's cold? Maybe I should knit him a scarf or something.

Doom-shroom

Doom-shroom can destroy **tons** of zombies at once—though he leaves behind a **massive** crater that you can't plant anything on and looks a real ~~stinky~~ mess. I suggest that if you survive the zombie attack, you should fill the crater with water and turn it into a pond.

Maybe get some goldfish?

Lily Pad

If you have a **pool** or a pond, plant a Lily Pad—then you can grow non-water-loving plants on top.

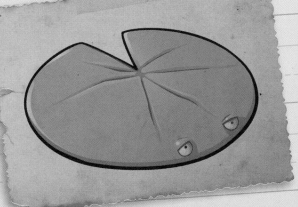

It's pretty much like a plant version of a boat. A green boat, made out of plants. I hereby name this ship **SS Leafy**. May God bless her and all who sail in her.

Squash

The Squash has short range, but does a **ton** of damage to any zombies that shuffle too close. Squash will squash the first zombie that gets in his way. It has great squash **skills** that it learned at the University of Squashing while getting a **degree** in Advanced Squash Studies.

Threepeater

This guy has **great** range and shoots peas in three lanes at once. Apart from that he's just like regular Peashooter, although **unlike** Peashooter he likes to read ▮▮▮▮▮ **books** in the quiet times when he's not helping you defeat zombies.

Tangle Kelp

Tangle Kelp lives in **water** and will pull in the first zombie that gets near it. I'm not sure what happens then, as zombies don't need to bre~~ath~~athe. Maybe it just talks to him for ages? Or maybe they just sit there in **silence**, looking at each other, waiting for **the end**.

Jalapeño

Jalapeño is a spicy number. When he **explodes**, he destroys all the zombies in his lane. I imagine he says something like "Que pase un buen día!" when he blows up. That means, "have a nice day." Spanish was the only school subject I was any good at.

That was probably because they let me wear a sombrero during class.

Spikeweed

Spikeweed hurts zombies' feet (that'll teach them not to wear **shoes**) and will also burst tires, if a zombie turns up driving a vehicle. Zombies also hate how he tastes so they won't eat him.

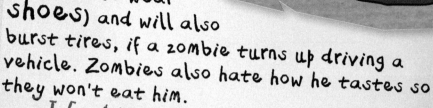

I feel the same way about fruit.

Torchwood

This guy turns peas that pass through him into **flaming peas** that do double the damage. Who knew hot peas could be so ~~w~~**dangerous?** I'll be sure to exercise extreme caution next time he's around peas. Torchwood looks pretty **angry**, but I guess that's 'cause he's on fire all the time.

Being on fire all the time would put anyone in a bad mood.

Tall-nut

Tall-nut is a taller version of Wall-nut, so he's good at defending your plants, even from zombies that can jump or vault. **Take that** zombies! They won't be so smug with their jumping skills when they get a face full of Tall-nut.

Sea-shroom

This is the aquatic version of a Puff-shroom. He might be called a Sea-shroom, but he lives in your pool. It makes me **sad** that I've never seen the sea. **Maybe** one day, when this is all over, me and Sea-shroom can take a trip to the seaside.

Plantern

If it's dark and foggy, Plantern is your man. Or plant. **Whatever**, stop trying to confuse me with your labels. This is exac**t**ly why I was asked to leave a restaurant that one time. If you're going to have **really** vague signs up on the doors, then you have to expect people to use the **wrong** bathroom.

Cactus

The Cactus shoots **spikes**, which is good. It can even shoot spikes in the air, which is even better if there are balloon zombies about. Why would a zombie be in a **balloon**? Well, it's a real nice way to get a better view of your brains.

Blover

These guys blow away **fog** and **balloon zombies**. They're also pretty handy to have on a hot day, as they can blow a nice **cool breeze** into your face. I also use them to cool down a cup of coffee if it's too hot, or to blow out the **candles** on my birthday cake if I'm out of breath or **can't be bothered.**

Help!

We went to a costume party dressed as **zombies** and now there are **real** zombies around. Can we come inside your house and **hide?**

Yours sincerely,

normal people (not zombies)

Starfruit

Quick to recharge, Starfruit shoots **stars** in five different direktions. Those directions are: north, east, south, west, and north-ish. See? I'm an **expert** at map directions as well as plants.

I'm clearly a useful guy to have around in an apocalypse, even if I do say so myself. . . .

Pumpkin

You can use Pumpkin to protect any plants you grow **inside** him. He's tough and **scary**, but don't let that put you off getting to know him better—his insides make a **great** soup or **pie**. Just don't mention that to him or you'll **never** be friends.

Magnet-shroom

Magnet-shroom removes **metal** things the zombies carry, like ladders, pickaxes, helmets, and trash cans. It could ~~metal~~ probably even steal the **fillings** out of a zombie's mouth. I'm not sure though.

Do I look like some kind of zombie dentist to you?

Cabbage-pult

This guy **hurls** cabbages at zombies. You'll often find him on the roof, though I'm **not sure** why. Maybe he's trying to adjust the satellite dish to get a better picture, or maybe he's checking for **Santa** and the reindeer. **Who knows?**

It's a crazy world we live in.

Flower Pot

Like the Lily Pad in the pool, Flower Pot lets you plant on the **roof**. Handy eh? I once tried to plant on the roof **without** Flower Pot, but I ended up with so much soil on the roof that it **collapsed**.

My bed ended up buried in earth and I had to sleep in a cupboard.

Kernel-pult

Kernel-pult lobs **corn** and **butter** at the zombies. Sounds like all the ingredients needed for a corny-buttery-zombie **party!** I don't know to be honest. I don't get **invited** to parties much these days (everyone seems to be a **zombie**).

Coffee Bean

Coffee isn't just for waking me up in the morning—it also wakes up ~~zom~~ mushrooms during the day. I usually make my own coffee at home. One time I went to some **fancy** coffee place and got real **confused** about what I was supposed to order. I ended up drinking **coffee** out of a can.

Garlic

If you've got a ton of zombies in one lane, plant some Garlic. When zombies eat him, they make an "ewwwwwwwwwwW" face and go into other lanes. **Pretty handy** to have around, though I wouldn't want to live with ~~a~~ stinky Garlic. I would have to wear a clothes-pin over my nose **all the time.**

Umbrella Leaf

This guy provides **more** than just shade. Umbrella Leaf protects other plants around him from Bungee Zombies and **basketballs**. The shade thing is pretty **handy** too though. I should know. Last time I fell asleep in the sun, I woke up looking like a **lobster**. My hands had turned into claws and I had a **shell!** Then I woke up and realized it was just a terrible dream.

Marigold

The Marigold chucks out **gold** and **silver** coins. The bad thing is that it can take ages to get around to it. Maybe Marigold is too busy reading the bu~~ll~~siness section in the newspaper, or checking share prices. Or maybe Marigold just likes **thinking** about coins?

Melon-pult

The Melon-pult lobs watermelons at zombies, which **squish** on impact (the watermelon, not the zombies, duh-uh) and do heavy damage to zombies nearby. It's also fast, which has given Melon-pult a bit of a **big ego** if you ask me. It's all "I'm the **greatest**" or "I do so much **damage,** look at me." Melon-pult needs to learn modesty **in my opinion.**

Gatling Pea

The Gatling Pea is an 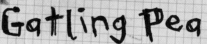 upgrade for the Repeater and fires **four** peas at the same time. That's a **lot** of peas. If you left the Gatling Pea alone for a couple of hours, you would have enough peas to fill my car. I know this for a fact, because I now have a car **full of peas.**

Twin Sunflower

This guy gives out **twice** as much sun as normal Sunflower. That's cool and everything, but I find twins a bit **creepy** to be honest. It's like they're two people. Other things I find ~~M~~creepy are **clowns** and most **puddings**.

Gloom-shroom

Gloom-shroom fires out heavy **fumes** in all directions, but the fumes don't go far. They also have to be planted on a Fume-shroom to work —take my **word** for this.

I once tried planting a Gloom-shroom in one of my **shoes** and all I got was a shoe full of ~~███~~ **dirt**.

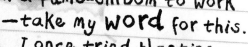

I still wear the shoe though. Dirt is nice.

Cattail

Cattail is an upgrade for the Lily Pad and can **shoot** at zombies in any lane. Even **Balloon** Zombies! Don't be **fooled** by the "cat" part of his name and the fact he looks like a cat. Cattail **won't** drink a saucer of milk, or play with a ball of yarn. In fact, Cattail makes me re-evaluate **everything** I thought I knew about cats.   And **tails**.

Winter Melon

Like the Melon-pult, Winter Melon does **heavy damage** to zombies. And because this guy is frozen, he also **slows** zombies down. You have to plant him on a **Melon-pult** though, because he likes to be near his friends.

I wish Winter Melon had more self-confidence.

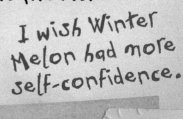

Gold Magnet

This guy is an **upgrade** from the Magnet-shroom. Gold Magnet collects **coins** and **diamonds** for you, which frees your time up to do other things. Other things I like to do include thinking about **stuff** and eating **stuff**.

Spikerock

Spikerock is an upgrade from **Spikeweed** and will **burst** tires and **hurt zombies' feet**. Nothing hurts zombies' feet more than Spikerock, except making them walk for **miles** and miles in shoes that **don't** ⚡⚡⚡ **fit** properly.

Or maybe making cruel jokes about their **mothers**.

Cob Cannon

Cob Cannon is another upgrade. **Hooray!** Plant him side-by-side with two Kernel-pults. He's slow to recharge and fire, but does **massive** damage and can fire at **any** zombies. Despite all this, Cob Cannon is a really **nice guy** if you spend time getting to know him properly. Just don't let him read you any of his ~~bad~~ poetry.

Imitater

Imitater is a potato that can imitate any other plant. Apart from itself, obviously. That would be **silly**—a potato imitating a **potato?** That would just be a regular potato then. At least, I think so. Oh ~~no~~ boy, now you've made my brains hurt.

I was only trying to help you and now I have a headache.

Bonk Choy

During the Ming Dynasty, **ancestors** of Bonk Choy were studied by the Emperor's personal cabbage expert. They call him now what they called his ancestors—the **King of Cabbages!** Or sometimes the **Brassica Boss** (but I prefer the first one as I'm not sure what the other one means).

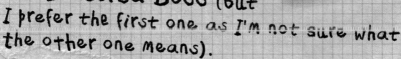

Coconut Cannon

Coconut Cannon just **loves** to help you defeat zombies. It really **makes his day.** It's all he thinks about. You may be asking why this hairy little guy is so **obsessed** with zombie **destruction?** The sad truth is that he's **empty** inside (once you've drunk the tasty milk that lurks within, that is).

Iceberg

Poor little Iceberg used to be friends with Snow Pea and Winter Melon. One evening the three of them went out for dinner and Winter Melon ordered a salad. Iceberg was sure that he knew some of the lettuce in the salad and got into a big argument with Winter Melon. Snow Pea just quietly pushed herself around the plate.

Snapdragon

Snapdragon thinks its name is off-putting to a lot of people—"snap" makes it sound grumpy, which it is not. It's lovely. Snapdragon has helpfully suggested some more friendly sounding names you can call it, like Dragonface or Petal-features.

I like to call it Trevor.

Spring Bean

Always full of **energy** and bounce, Spring Bean is a real early riser—he's always getting up at **dawn**. "The **early** bean catches the zombie trying to eat brains!" says Spring Bean. It's an odd saying, but exactly what do you expect from a **talking plant?**

Peapod

Peapod might **seem** like a catchy name, but it took a botanist guy **ages** to come up with it. I still think "**pea-cekeeper**," "**pea-chy**" or "**pea-nut**" would be better, but I suppose that's why **nobody** will let me be a botanist.

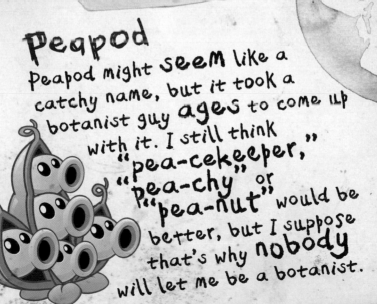

Explode-o-nut

He's a **rare** variety, but if you should come across the Explode-o-nut it's worth knowing what he does. He's basically a red version of Wall-nut that **explodes** like a Cherry Bomb when a zombie touches him. **Why** is he red? I think he's embarrassed about something, like forgetting to wear **pants** once when he left the **garden**.

Giant Wall-nut

Another **rare** variety, but good for **squishing** loads of zombies at once. Giant Wall-nut looks like a normal Wall-nut, but acts like a Squash and Jalapeño. He sounds like he has some kind of **crazy** mixed-up identity crisis, yeah?

Like that time when I put on a dress and made all the plants call me "Crazy Dave's Mom."

Bloomerang

Bloomerang **always** returns to you, no matter what! You can chuck him away but he **always** comes back. Even if you **hide**. Or go on vacation for a couple of weeks. Bloomerang is **dedicated** like that.

Chili Bean

Hey, hot stuff! I know you have a **debilitating flatulence problem**, but try not to let it get you down, OK? I've heard that some people out there actually quite like that awful bean bum smell. So cheer up and **let rip**, little smelly guy!

Grave Buster

If you plant a Grave Buster on a grave it gets rid of the grave. Simple, right? It may sound simple to you or me, but the other day I tried explaining it to my new best friend **Gary**. Gary just didn't ~~\#\#~~ get it, no matter how many times I explained.

Gary is a **chair** though, so maybe that's why.

Hi, thiz iz the **gaz man**. I have to come over and read your **gaz meter** and check for any **bad gaz smells**. Bad gaz smells are more **dangerous** than zombies, so can you let me in please? **Sincerely,**

gaz man

Power Lily

Power Lily is the best at doing what Power Lily does. But what Power Lily does is always refer to Power Lily in the third person. Power Lily drives the other plants crazy with that. But hey, it's Power Lily. What can they really do? Power Lily says: nothing.

Split Pea

Split Pea sees what you're doing. Even when you don't think he's looking, he's got his eye on you. You just watch your step, pal. He's like a fortune teller: sees all, knows all. And then sees some more.

Lightning Reed

There's an old saying that goes "Lightning never strikes twice." **THIS IS LIES.** Lightning Reed has been on strike at least fifteen times —often protesting about the poor treatment of reeds in the workplace, or the selection of **cookies** available to workers during coffee breaks.

Magnifying Grass

If you ask me, the problem with Magnifying Grass is that he's always making a **big deal** out of little things. He can't help it, he was **born** that way. When you're born with a magnifying talent you either make small things big, or focus the rays of the sun and **burn stuff.**

One thing you can do during the zombie apocalypse is keep a **diary**. A diary is good for remembering all the **fun** things that happen (not much fun stuff happens during an apocalypse) and all the zombies you meet (you meet a **ton** of zombies).

Maybe one day when this is all over, I'll get my diary out and read it and **laugh**.

Remember that time there was a zombie in a balloon? **Hahahaha!**

Remember that time a peashooter got a zombie in the eye? **Hohohohohoo!**

Remember that time the zombies went swimming and they almost ate my brains? **Hehehehehe!**

Remember that time all the **meat sandwiches** in the world had been eaten?

Then, a **single tear** will roll down my cheek at that sad thought. Nostalgia's a real mixed bag of emotions.

Crazy Dave's Apocalypse Diary

Monday

Woke up early. Like to wake up with the birds, though I find sharing a bed with the birds not always so great—they always hog the blankets and sometimes ~~and~~ poop everywhere (I'm talking about you, Mr. Seagull).

Got dressed, put saucepan on head and had breakfast—cereal.

Just Kidding! Had bacon for breakfast like usual. It's important to keep to a regular routine, even during zombie apo~~ll~~calypse.

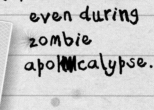

No zombies attacked today, which was nice of them.

Tuesday

Watered the **garden** this morning, but think I might be doing it wrong. None of the plants could open **any** of the bottles I left out for them. Do I have to do **everything** around here?

Went into town in the afternoon— found a kitchen shop. Tried on a few different **saucepan hats**, but not impressed with them. Decided to stick to my **regular** saucepan hat. It fits like a glove.

That gives me a great idea —what if I get small saucepans to wear as **gloves?** Would keep cold out in winter and stop zombies from nibbling on my fingers.

Wednesday

Still no zombies around.

It may sound crazy but I'm starting to **MISS** zombies. Zombies are like **friends**. Friends that mess up your garden, try to break into your house, and eat your **brains**. Wait a minute— I don't need friends like that!

Not when I have **real** friends, like **Mr. Seagull**.

the back of my face

Thursday

The weekend is almost here! I'm so happy! That said, the weekend is much like any other day in the zombie apocalypse, as people don't go to work anymore and have to watch out for zombies trying to eat their brains all the time.

Friday

Loads of zombies attacked today. Turns out they got **lost** on the way to my house and went to the **graveyard** instead.

A graveyard is like a **second home** to zombies. They can catch up with old friends, meet new zombies, and have **long** talks about brains and stuff. Actually, not stuff. Just **brains.** Wonder if conversations in graveyards get a bit **boring** sometimes?

Went to bed early. **Tired** from zombie attack. Plus, the earlier I go to bed, the sooner it is that I can wake up and eat breakfast.

Hi there,
    We don't like eating brains anymore
and would like to come over and say
    sorry. We even baked cookies!
    Please leave yoor front door open
so we can come in.
    Sincerely,
        Vegetarian zombies

Time-Killing Tips

Apart from the constant threat of having your brains **eaten**, the big threat during a zombie apocalypse is **boredom**. If boredom could shuffle around and get into your house and eat your brains it would be a **bigger** enemy than the zombies—but it can't. This is why I've put it **second** on my list of enemies. **Duh.**

"So, Crazy Dave," you ask me, **Crazy Dave.** "What other ways can I kill time?" The first way I tried to **kill time** was by bashing a clock with a **big rock,** but this only took a **few minutes** (actually, I'm not sure exactly how long it took, as the clock **stopped working** after I started bashing it).

Other ways I like to kill time:

1. Counting toes and fingers. Are they all there? Yes? That's real good!

2. Mowing the lawn. I like to roll around in all the fresh grass clippings. Good to have a hobby.

3. Looking at clouds. That cloud looks like a zombie! That other cloud looks like a zombie riding a horse! That cloud looks like two zombies kissing! That cloud looks like a zombie in a top hat going to the opera, or somewhere else really fancy where people expect you to wear top hats! Or maybe it just looks like a regular cloud.

4. Shouting at garbage cans. It's OK, garbage cans have really thick skins and don't mind being shouted at.

5. Spring cleaning. I have too many springs in my house and car. Good to throw them away (though many springs just bounce back, hee hee).

Of course, if these things don't appeal to you, you could always spend your time becoming an amazing scientist instead. If you do, you can be just like me and journey into the distant future! Woo woo woo!

Want to know more? Then take your first step into time and space by turning the page!

Crazy Dave's Guide to the Future?

Right. Now I want you to stop reading this book and wait thirty seconds.

Tick tock wait

Done that? Good—you just traveled into the future! How is it there? Tons of robots running around? Is your mom a hologram? Did you download your breakfast off the internet?

OK, so thirty-second future is pretty much the same as before you time-traveled—but I know what the distant future will be like, and now I shall tell you all about it because:

i) you probably won't live for thousands of years to see it (sorry)

ii) you don't have a time machine (more of that later)

FUTURE TECHNOLOGY

You think technology these days is pretty cool? Technology in the future will blow your mind. (They actually have a thing that blows your mind; it's a tiny fan you stick in your ear.)

Mobile Phones

In the future, phones are even smaller. They make your current phone look like you're carrying around a watermelon. Phones in the future are about the size of a grain of rice. The battery still runs out after a couple of hours though, and a phone that size is a nightmare to charge. You spend hours trying to plug the tiny cable in. Plus, ringtones are all still really ~~mean~~ annoying

Zombies in the Future

Yeah, they still have zombies in the future, but people have gotten used to them. It's like the first time you had broccoli and thought it was horrible, but then a few years later you get used to it and it's not so bad. So future zombies are like broccoli —both are green and . . . er, have stalks?

Hologram Sandwiches

In the future, they don't bother with actual food (real food is messy and spoils). Instead they have hologram food. Most people eat sandwiches in the form of a hologram that gets beamed into your hands. My favorite is the ham hologram sandwich, or holoham as I like to call it (though I seem to be the only one who does).

FUTURE TRANSPORT

People still have to go places in the future, but the way they get around has changed a lot.

Jetpacks

A popular way for future zombies to get around is by jetpack. Zombies really aren't that smart though, so most of them end up setting their feet on fire from the jetpack's flames. That's OK though, because someone invented fireproof shoes. They think of everything in the future!

Big Train

It's like the trains we have now, but three times the scale. I guess it's so that everyone can get a seat and it's not so crowded, but everything is like three times bigger so it's really hard to get up and into the seats. You need a ladder.

Mega Jumpy Boots

Instead of you going somewhere, the Mega Jumpy Boots make the place come to you. Basically, you jump really high up in the air and only come back down when the earth has turned around enough to get where you're going. Now that I think about it, a huge train with a ladder doesn't sound so stupid after all.

FUTURE ENTERTAINMENT

In the future, people enjoy **weird** entertainment. They don't watch TV or movies any more, but prefer to be entertained by a half-robot, half-zombie, half-something-else. **Hold on** ... that's one and a half things. I guess that's value for the money!

Robot Disco Zombie

Sometimes, people want to **dance** for some reason. But they don't dance in the future—they watch a Robot Disco Zombie dance instead. He's a pretty good dancer, but I don't know if that's because of the zombie bit or the robot bit. It's definitely **not** the disco bit. Nothing good **ever** came from disco.

Interplanetary Communiqué Deployer

Evil Cat Declawing Device

Thingamajig

Belgian Waffle Maker

Mech Accountant

Not every idea they have in the future is a good one. They can't all be **holoham** sandwiches! Sometimes in the future, people like to watch a Mech Accountant. He's basically half-robot, half-accountant, and he just **sits there** at his desk tapping on a calculator and nodding.

Crazy Dave's Time Machine

All this talk of the future isn't just Crazy Dave talking **crazy**. I'm not stupid you know. (OK, maybe I'm a bit **slow** first thing in the morning before I've had my coffee.) The reason I can talk so confidently about the future is that **I can go there!** I could go to the past too, but it's all in black and white and looks kinda **boring**.

So how do I travel to the future? In my **time-traveling motorhome thing** of course! How else do you think I'd travel through time? In a **phone booth?** Phone booths don't have toilets, comfy seats, TVs, or taco storage areas—and I like to time-travel in **style** (with tacos).

In this next section, I'm going to explain how my time machine works, the basic ideas behind time travel and my very own basic ground rules (**good to know** if I ever give you a lift to the future).

Flashing lights/sirens
Get out of my way, I'm traveling through time, WHOOOO HOOOOO! That's what I'd say if I was being silly. Good thing I'm a very serious, clever man with no time for being silly.

Satellite dish
An essential device for sending and receiving messages. Oh, and it also gets awesome TV—over 700 channels! My favorite is the one where they show close-up shots of a lamb kebab thingy going round and round and round and round.

Fast-food snack tray
Time travel makes you hungry, so you need somewhere to keep your food. OK, so it's not just the time travel that does it. I happen to have a really high metabolism, all right?

Fire extinguisher
In case everything in the future is on fire.

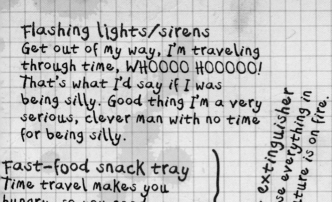

Rubber ring
In case it's really wet in the future.

Tires
Extra-thick tires to make sure you can stick to the roads. Who knows what roads will be made out of in the future? Probably lasers or something.

Stereo
When you get to the future, one way to impress future-people is with some cool music from our time. It sounds really retro and old to them—and we all know retro stuff is cool, right?

Giga time travel engine
To be honest, the time travel engine I designed and built is really small. I just think this thing looks cool.

Time Travel In A Nutshell

OK, so time travel sounds like it should be really complicated, but I promise it's not. It works like this:

An Einstein-Rosen Bridge (or wormhole) is a feature of spacetime that is a "shortcut" through space and time. A wormhole—created by folding space—is much like a tunnel with two ends, each in separate points in spacetime, allowing travel between those two points.

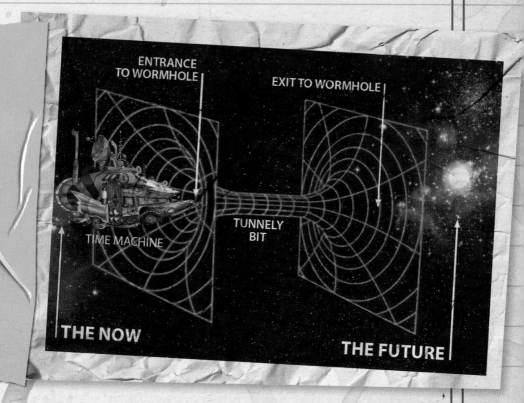

ENTRANCE TO WORMHOLE

EXIT TO WORMHOLE

TIME MACHINE

TUNNELY BIT

THE NOW

THE FUTURE

See? It's not that complicated. Sheesh!

What? You still don't get it? OK, it's basically like when you have **laundry** and you fold the laundry and then when you're done you realize you're now five minutes into the future. So it's like that, but with **more** laundry. And you're in a motorhome going really fast.

Time Machine Rules

1. **Take your shoes off** when you board. Have some respect! I hate dirty carpets.

2. **No touching the taco storage area.** This is precious stuff—who knows if they have tacos in the future?

3. When we get to the future, if you see your future self, **don't try to high-five yourself.** I think the universe might stop.

4. **Don't adjust the levels on the stereo.** I like bass. When you get your own time-traveling car/house you can adjust the stereo all you want, OK?

5. **Don't open the windows** when we're traveling through time (it smells weird in hyperspace).

TV!

It's TV Time!

Of course you (you being reading-this-book-person) don't have to go on an incredible voyage into the future to have fun. Sometimes it's good to just sit back and chill. When not gardening and stopping zombies, I'm one chilly guy.

Sometimes, I just stare at stuff, like hedges or clumps of dirt or the sink. But my favorite thing to stare at is a blank TV. It's just like watching regular TV, but you get to make up the shows that are on it. Much better! And it's helpful in an apokkkcalypse when all the TV people have stopped working because they're busy being zombies. This is what a typical night of great shows I like to imagine on my TV looks like:

126

STRICTLY DANCING AND BRAINS

7PM: ZOMBIE HOSPITAL

This a **really good** hospital drama where all the doctors and patients are zombies. You get real insight into the lives of the people who work at Zombie Hospital, though they never really make anyone better. They just eat **brains**, or walk around the hospital looking for brains. Actually this show is kinda boring.

8PM: MY BIG FAT ANTIQUE BRAINS

Every week zombies bring along really old brains, then expert zombies tell them how much the brains are worth. Zombies don't understand or use money though, so all the brains end up getting eaten. I can't imagine old brains taste good. Maybe they get cured, like ham?

8.30PM: THE BRAIN GAME

The world's favorite game show! Except for "Who Wants to Eat Some Brains?" obviously.

9PM: ZOMBIE FRIENDS

Hilarious comedy show about bunch of twenty something zombies living in the big city. My favorite episode is when the stupid zombie eats a brain sandwich (**off the floor!**) and the nerdy zombie asks a girl out, then eats her brains.

9.30PM: BRAIN NEWS

It is **pretty important** to keep up with all the latest news on brains—who has got brains, how many brains are left, etc.

10PM: APOCALYPSE NOOOOOOOOOOOOO!

Movie time! This film is basically just a bunch of people standing around going "nooooooooooooo!" because there is a zombie apocalypse. It's pretty good, but I hope they don't make a sequel or anything.

127

Hi there, son/daughter.

This is a note from your Muther,
who is a nice lady and NOT a zombie.
I would really like to visit you soon.
Please don't plant things on the lawn
and leave your front door open. I will
give you a big hug.

Love, Mom x

One of my favorite things about wandering around with nothing to do is that I get to pick stuff up off the ground and keep it forever. And, because there's hardly anyone else around any more, it means there's no one to shout "ewwww" or cross to the other side of the street. Or call the ~~police~~ police. Now I'm putting my prize collection on display for the first time ever! I'm calling this exhibition . . .

SOME STUFF I FOUND ON THE STREET

Please, step into my gallery (remember to take your shoes off first).

Leaf

Shopping List

3 shovels
bandages
large knife
30 large bottles water
Gas stove
450 cans beans
1 can rice pudding
2 x magazines

BUNNY SUIT ZOMBIE

130

PACO'S TACOS
YOU'LL GO WACKO FOR OUR TACOS!!!

BUY ELEVEN OF OUR DELICIOUS TACOS AND GET HALF OF YOUR TWELFTH TACO ABSOLUTELY FREE!

Available while stocks last. Offer not open to zombies or vegetarians. Sorry about that.

FRANKEN-ZOMBIE

SHUFFLERS

Brain & Vinegar
Potato Crisps

NOT TO BE SOLD SEPARATELY, OR AT ALL

131

More
Leaves

COOKING ZOMBIE

Kiss
the
Cook

HELP

MASKED VIGILANTE ZOMBIE

University of Morticultural Sciences

Upon the recommendation of the faculty
hereby confers on

Edgar George Zomboss

the Degree of

Doctor of Thanatology

for promising to take his giant killer robot
and never come back.

Judith O'Day
Dean

TUXEDO ZOMBIE

hELLO i am CRAZy DAVE

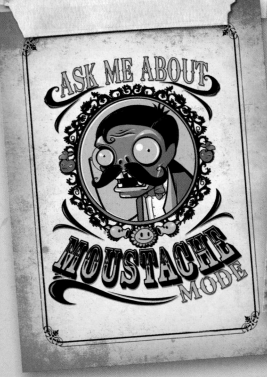

ASK ME ABOUT

MOUSTACHE MODE

CHOMPER

Hallo neighbor,
we are **new** to the area and would like to come over to your house for pizza. When we say pizza we mean pizza, **not** brainz.
Looking forward to eating meeting you!
Sincerely,
your new non-zombie neighbors

Thankyou so much!

GARDENER OF THE YEAR

ROLLER ZOMBIE

SCRATCH 'N SNIFF
(we dare you.)

137

MY TOWN

I live in the same town I grew up in. It used to be a nice town, but since the zombies took over it's not been as great as it used to be. I guess the potential for having your brains eaten any minute of the day can really ruin the atmosphere of a place. Some people can be really sensitive about that kind of thing.

Another thing about my town is that since this whole zombie apo**N**calypse thing happened, I can't help but notice that we don't get as many **tourists** as we used to. So I decided to make a tourism **leaflet** in the hope that folks don't just write us off as another "zombie-infested town where I'm bound to get my brains eaten."

Maybe **this** will convince people to hang around and see the sights? Maybe even buy a **souvenir!**

You've not really visited a town full of
zombies until you've visited ...

Neighborville

Come for the zombies, stay for the garden
gnome we have! It's really cool.

BROUGHT TO YOU IN ASSOCIATION WITH
Crazy Dave's Crazy Tacos*
*Tacos not actually crazy.
(Unless crazy delicious counts!)

Why not take some time out to visit some of these exciting and memorable landmarks?

Crazy Davington Castle

Ahhh, a magical place full of memories. This is where I grew up. In fact, my mom has kept my bedroom exactly the same ever since I moved out. To be fair, my room was actually a damp corner of the basement so I don't blame her for not going down there much.

Bread Heads

"You want bread? They got bread! Unless the baker's dead." Hmmm, I was trying to come up with a new slogan for the bakery, but I don't think that's quite right. "Don't be an oaf, buy a loaf!" Better?

Well, Well, Well

If you're in town and you get
thirsty, why not get a cool,
crisp, refreshing bucket of
water from the town well? Just
be sure to check the bucket
for bits of zombies that might
have dropped off and fallen
in there. Garnishes cost extra!

Hungry Helper

The town market sells all kinds of
local produce like bread, milk, and cheese.
It also has a flat roof, which is the perfect place
to escape to if you
get surrounded by
a horde of zombies
while buying bread,
milk, and cheese. You
don't see that level of
service in your fancy
big city supermarkets!

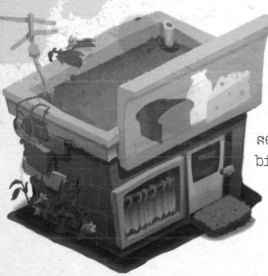

Hair to the Throne

Make sure you look your best while visiting by getting a haircut from the town barber. Just check that the barber isn't one of the undead before you sit in the chair, otherwise it might be more than your hair that gets trimmed. (I'm talking about a zombie eating your brains here, OK?)

Emilie's Everything Emporium

Why not pick up a memento of your visit at our store? This place sells everything! Well OK, not everything. For example, they don't sell helicopters made out of pork. Who would buy that? Actually, I would.

Plantastic!

Ask any of the (surviving) residents of our town and they'll tell you that plants are the most important things to them. That's mostly because they stop the zombies, though the plants do also look nice. Except maybe Melon-pult. He looks terrible. Ha ha, only joking, Melon-pult!

The Trash Can

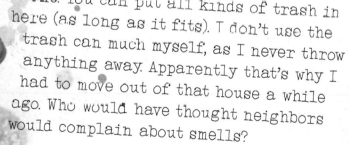

We might only have one trash can in our town, but it's a good one. You can put all kinds of trash in here (as long as it fits). I don't use the trash can much myself, as I never throw anything away. Apparently that's why I had to move out of that house a while ago. Who would have thought neighbors would complain about smells?

Garden Gnome

One of the undisputed highlights of the town is the garden gnome. You simply must come and see him. Seriously, you have to. I think a wizard put a curse on him years ago and anyone who doesn't ask the gnome's permission to visit the town gets turned into a golden hen. I think. Maybe that milk I drank this morning had gone bad? I feel odd.

Pink Flamingo

He might look like a real pink flamingo that stands on your lawn and never moves, but guess what? He's not real! He's made out of plastic! You can stare at him for hours expecting him to move, but he doesn't! Yeah, you don't get those kind of thrills in your fancy theme parks, do you?

Even Our Trees Are Friendly!

If there's one thing I love, it's a massive tuna sandwich with loads of mustard. But if there's ANOTHER thing I love, it's trees with happy, smiley faces. Sometimes I think I'd like to climb up into them and give them a big leafy hug, and let them tell me that everything is going to be all right. I've never seen an unhappy-looking tree—not even in the winter time when their leaves fall off and they end up all cold and bashful.

Taking Care of Your Garden

You know I love gardening, right? The garden is where you get to keep all the plants you've made friends with. You can't just leave them alone and hope for the best (I did that with a pet goldfish once and I'm still **really sorry** about it to this day). Plants need water, bug spray, and music to grow up all good and **nice**.

Sometimes I like to talk to my plants, though the plants **never** talk back. Sometimes I'm pretty sure I can hear plants **whispering** though.

Why are you so **shy**, plants? You and I have been through so much together. It's not like when I talk to Couch. I don't **expect** Couch to talk back.

But sometimes it does and I have to leave the room for a while.

You need gardening **gloves** or a **wheelbarrow** to move plants around. I like to move plants around sometimes. It's fun for them. I think they appreciate a different view once in a while—like taking a little **vacation**.

Once plants are fully grown, they start making coins for you, which is good. Then you can buy more plants and stuff. Don't buy them **sandwiches** though—sandwiches are precious and most plants (even Coffee Beans) don't **appreciate** them. Not in the way I appreciate them, anyway.

If you ever need help with your garden, you should ask **Stinky the Snail.** Stinky is a bit slow and he leaves really weird **slimy** stuff everywhere he goes, but his heart's in the right place. I don't mention the slime problem to him. Do you think maybe I **should** so that he will see a doctor?

Congratulations,

you haf won a big prize in a lottery you didn't know you entered! Please leave your front door OPEN so we can give you your moneys.

Sincerely,

guy from the lottery

Crazy Dave's Lookbook

By now you've probably noticed a few things about me:
- I'm pretty smart (you remember my awesome gardening/time travel skills, right?)
- I'm really handsome (oh you, making me blush!)
- I'm really, really fashionable.

Yep, I am one trendy guy. I'd like you to look as good as I do—which is why I've put together this "lookbook" with my style tips so no one confuses you with a badly dressed zombie.

Spring/Summer Look

Hat: Perfect for protecting you against unexpected rain showers and/or zombie attacks. This non-stick headwear is the perfect blend of modern and avant-garde.

Beard: A beard in summer? Yes! This makes a clear statement, which is: "This beard may be really hot and itchy in the summer, but I'm willing to suffer for fashion. And I'm too lazy to shave."

Shirt: This deceptively simple cotton affair shows off my figure, with a generous cut that's perfect for balmy summer evenings spent avoiding zombies.

Belt: This choice in waist-wear really sets me apart as a style icon, making me the talking point of fashionistas everywhere (or at least I would be if they hadn't all had their brains eaten).

Jeans: Denim is in this season. These dark jeans are both tough and long-lasting. It's also the right color to hide any stains from salsa, ketchup, or soil.

Shoes: The sneaker is the must-have choice of footwear in the summer. Perfect for a light jog to escape a single shuffling zombie, or essential for running like crazy when chased by a ravenous zombie horde.

Autumn/Winter Look

Hat: Perfect for keeping out rain, snow, or the chomping teeth of a hungry zombie. This daring choice tells people that the wearer likes to keep their brains safe, but can also do basic cooking.

Beard: Ginger facial fuzz is hot this season. It reflects the changing colors of leaves as the cold nights approach. It's also good at catching any cornflakes that I don't eat, making it the perfect blend of form and function.

Shirt: Boldly setting a statement in casual wear, this "shirt" is clearly the new "shirt."

Belt: This choice of belt is guaranteed to turn heads —especially if it snaps and my pants fall down.

Jeans: This leg-wear is an edgy choice this season, but also suggests the wearer is willing to break fashion rules with a "just thrown on" look. Mainly because I did just throw them on (I sometimes sleep in my car and there's no room for a wardrobe).

Shoes: I like these sneakers because they are truly multi-purpose. They're not just footwear! They can be used to keep a large bottle of soda upright or—in a pinch—can function as a pair of mittens.

Crazy Dave's Twiddydinkies Catalogue

You know how people love vans that sell **burgers** and ice cream? Well, that was my idea. Only I don't sell burgers from a van—I sell seeds, upgrades, and defenses from the back of my **car**. And what do I call this wondrous business? **Twiddydinkies!** Hurray!

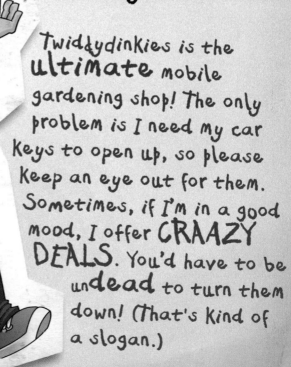

Twiddydinkies is the **ultimate** mobile gardening shop! The only problem is I need my car keys to open up, so please keep an eye out for them. Sometimes, if I'm in a good mood, I offer CRAAZY DEALS. You'd have to be un**dead** to turn them down! (That's kind of a slogan.)

Twiddydinkies is not the first shop I have had. One time I used to have a shop selling balloon animals. I made all kinds of animals out of **balloons** (mostly poodles and sausage dogs) to sell to **everyone** in town. But it turns out you can only sell so many balloon animals before everyone has one, then they don't want them any more. When that happened I had to close up shop **forever.**

I guess I'm a better gardener than I am a businessman-tycoon type.

Crazy Dave's CRAZY Deals

I don't just have lots of great advice to offer. I also sell some great **non-garden-type** stuff. Since there's not so many people around anymore, there's even more **stuff** for everyone to have!

Hey look, I gotta make a living! Bacon doesn't grow on trees you know. If it did I would have a **forest** of bacon trees. Maybe some maple trees as well to get syrup to go with all that bacon. Are **fried egg trees** also a thing yet? If not, why not?

Anyway, here is some other stuff I'm selling. If you want to buy any of it let me know. Maybe leave a note under my car's windshield wipers?

MYSTERY BAG $49.99

What's inside the **Mystery Bag?** I don't know, I can't be bothered to look inside. It's probably something cool though. Or it's empty.

SCREEN DOORS $15.99

I have a bunch of **screen doors** in my garden. Maybe you could turn them into something else, like a coffee table or a really leaky boat?

ONE PAIR OF PANTS $29.99

Previous owner "A. Zombie." Pants are in good condition. Still have **both** legs inside!

154

CRAZY DAVE'S STORY TIME $9 (per hour)

If you get bored I can come over to your house and tell you a story. I have a **ton** of great stories. Pretty much all the stories involve **SOME FORM OF SANDWICH**, but if you don't like sandwiches I won't come over to your house no matter how much money you pay me.

SHOPPING CART $19.99

I have a car, so I've already got a way of getting around town (as long as I can find the keys). Maybe you could use this **shopping cart?** Good for going down hills, not so good for bumpy ground or going up hills. Or going around in the lake.

BIG PILES O' STUFF

$29.99

I have a ton of big piles of **stuff** everywhere, so I'm selling most of them. They make my garden look **untidy**. Not sure what the stuff is, but you should buy it. Less questions and more spending please!

If you have been injured in a custard-related incident:

    i) Wipe a towel over the custard stain or spill.

    ii) Wait until it gets better.

    iii) Relax.

IF YOU DO NOT HAVE A TOWEL AT HAND

Gather leaves and twigs from the garden, then knit together a crude patchwork towel from them.
By the time you've finished doing this, the medical emergency will probably be over and you'll have looked really busy doing something. Success!

3. DURING THE ZOMBIE ATTACK

In this section of the book, we aim to answer such important questions as:

> *How will I know when zombies are coming?*
> *Am I under attack?*
> *What should I do?*
> *Have my brains been eaten?*
> ~~*Is it OK to eat cheese before bedtime?*~~

Many different scenarios can unfold during a zombie attack. You may be presented with a number of options at any time—we recommend you think each one through carefully. Or toss a coin. Or close your eyes. Just do something quickly—zombies are attacking!

Think through the following scenarios and see what you would do in that situation. Then, when you've finished reading this section come back to this page and see if you would do things differently.

Scenario #1—Zombie interrupts play

You are attending a baseball game when a zombie strays onto the field with the sole intent of eating the batter's brains. How do you react?

a) Loudly berate the zombie by yelling "You, Sir, are not a good sport!"

b) Run away.

c) Try to lure the zombie off the field with a plate of cookies.

Scenario #2—Zombie on the bus

You are taking the bus home when a zombie gets on at a stop not far from your house. What do you do?

a) Complain to the driver that the zombie hasn't paid for a ticket.

b) Run away.

c) Pay for the zombie's ticket out of courtesy.

Scenario #3—Zombie movie

You are watching the latest blockbuster Hollywood movie at the theater. A zombie is standing in front of the screen, blocking your view. What do you do?

a) Ask for your money back when the film is over.

b) Run away.

c) Politely offer the zombie some of your popcorn.

How Will I Know When the Zombies Are Coming?

When the Government is aware that zombies are approaching your neighborhood, we will sound an alarm, officially known as UNGA (Undead Nearness General Alert). When you hear the UNGA, listen for the number of times it sounds:

One long blast followed by three short blasts
Zombies have been spotted nearby. Go inside your home at once.

One long blast followed by two short blasts, followed by another long blast
Zombies have been spotted, but they are still far away. You have plenty of time to finish that cup of tea you just made.

One long blast, followed by five short blasts and two long blasts, and then another short blast
One zombie has been spotted nearby. Or possibly it's someone in costume.

One long blast, followed by ten short blasts, then three long blasts, four short blasts, two long blasts, six short blasts, then a kind of "toot" sound
The man operating the UNGA is clearly bored and has taken to fooling around with the alarm to pass the time.

As we're neighbors, you should also listen out for me shouting. Unless I've just dropped something heavy on my foot obviously—then the shouting won't be about zombies.

Am I Under Attack? A Flow Chart

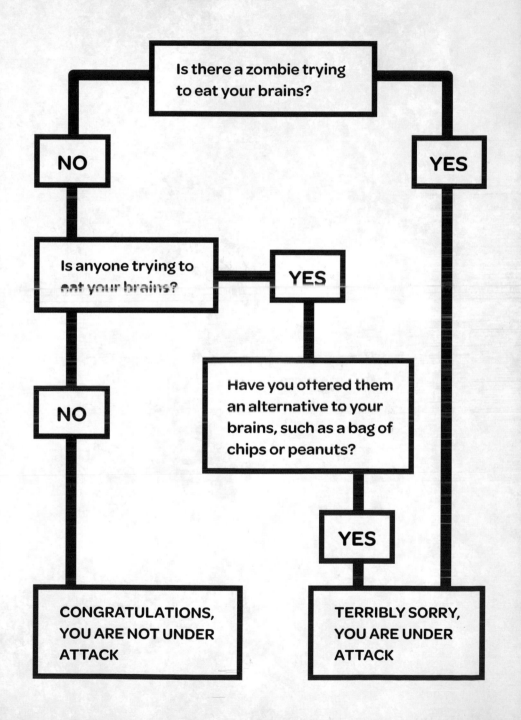

Is there a zombie trying to eat your brains?

NO

YES

Is anyone trying to eat your brains?

YES

NO

Have you offered them an alternative to your brains, such as a bag of chips or peanuts?

YES

CONGRATULATIONS, YOU ARE NOT UNDER ATTACK

TERRIBLY SORRY, YOU ARE UNDER ATTACK

What to Do If You're at Home When the Zombies Come

Your house is the safest place to be if you hear UNGA or spot a zombie near your home. If you find yourself in a zombie situation at home, take the following steps immediately:

 Lock all doors and windows. Then unlock all doors and windows and lock them again, to be doubly sure.

 Nail large pieces of crooked wood over the windows. The zombies can easily break through this, but it'll make you feel better.

 Put the kettle on.

 Turn on the radio and listen for news. Or a good song to dance around the kitchen to.

 Fill the bath with water. This will be your supply of drinking water during the zombie apocalypse, or it may come in handy if you need a refreshing cold bath to wake yourself up.

 If you are with family and/or friends, high-five everyone in order to keep spirits up. If you are alone, high-five yourself.

 Turn off the electricity. This means you will not be able to watch your favorite television programs, but this is one of the many inconveniences of the apocalypse you will have to deal with.

If the zombies are directly outside your home:

It is time to head to your ZITS (refer to pages 58-61).

What to Do If You're Out When the Zombies Come

As previously stated, being at home is the safest place to be during a zombie attack. But we understand that you can't always be at home all of the time. Sometimes you need to go to the store to buy milk, or mail a letter—or just get some fresh air with a nice walk.

Sadly, zombie attacks will result in this "nice" walk becoming the single most terrifying experience of your life (should you be lucky enough to survive it). Please DO NOT blame your Government for ruining your walk. Blame the zombies. If you are out when a zombie attack occurs, take the following steps immediately:

 Take cover by flinging yourself down on the ground, no matter where you are. This action is made much more comfortable if you are in a mattress store, so try to plan a visit to a mattress store whenever you leave the house, just in case.

 Cover your head. This may be with a pillow (ideal if you are in the mattress store as described above) or with your hands. This will help protect your brains from the lazier members of the zombie community.

HeelllloooooooOo. Did I not mention the saucepan-hat already? Why use hands?

 If you are lying on the ground, try digging down into the soil. Or, for extra safety, try wearing a shirt with a realistic picture of some grass on the back. Zombies may think you are just a lump on the lawn and pass you by.

 If the zombies pass you by, be sure to ask yourself the question "Am I a zombie?" (see *Have My Brains Been Eaten?* on pages ~~84-85~~ 172–173

If you are sure the zombie danger has passed:

Complete your walk, buy your milk, or mail your letter—then proceed home and let out a loud sigh of relief.

Top 10 Hiding Places

If the zombie apocalypse has caught you unprepared and you do not have ZITS handy, or perhaps you do not want to fling yourself on the ground (maybe it has been raining and you don't want to get mud on your clothes), another option is to hide.

Our scientists have compiled the following list of suggested hiding places and the likely outcome of using them.

1. **Behind a tree**
    You may choose to hide from zombie hordes behind a tree. Make sure there are no dogs around if you do this, or the situation could get tricky.
    LIKELY OUTCOME: Attacked by zombies.

2. **Under a big pile of jewelry**
    You could wear so much jewelry that zombies may not see you. The downside of this is becoming very heavy, expensive, and shiny.
    LIKELY OUTCOME: Attacked by zombies.

3. **In an abandoned car**
    You may come across an abandoned car to hide in. Just make sure you check the backseat for zombies first.
    LIKELY OUTCOME: Attacked by zombies (people *never* check the backseat for zombies).

4. **Behind a cow**
    If you live in the countryside, you may be able to hide behind a cow. Be aware that the cow may run away, as they notoriously don't like being used as hiding places.
    LIKELY OUTCOME: Attacked by zombies and/or people looking for milk.

5. Inside a mailbox

While a mailbox can accommodate a person hiding from zombies, you also run the risk of getting letters in your face.

LIKELY OUTCOME: Attacked by zombies, getting paper cuts.

6. Under a bed

Hiding under a bed may seem like a good idea, but there is often a lot of dust underneath beds, which will make you sneeze.

LIKELY OUTCOME: Attacked by zombies, or at the very least you'll call attention to yourself by sneezing.

7. In a cupboard

If you choose to hide in a cupboard, make sure it is not full of stationery (pens, paper, etc.). Zombies like to write notes so a stationery cupboard is the first place they will head to.

LIKELY OUTCOME: Attacked by zombies.

8. Behind a tea bag

This is silly. Why would you do this? And why did over twenty of our top scientists do this? Perhaps they weren't as clever as we thought.

LIKELY OUTCOME: Attacked by zombies.

9. Behind a pile of onions

While onions might make us non-zombies cry, they do not have the same effect on zombies, as zombies do not have tear ducts. Even when they don't get to have brains for dinner they don't cry. Zombies are emotionally undead.

LIKELY OUTCOME: Attacked by zombies.

10. Inside your own imagination

We do not recommend this. One of our scientists closed his eyes and imagined he was somewhere else, like a sunny zombie-free beach.

LIKELY OUTCOME: Attacked by zombies.

Be Ready to Run

If your home, ZITS, or hiding place is compromised, you may need to run away from any attacking zombie horde. If this happens, you should have an escape route worked out, so you can get to a safe(ish) place quickly and avoid having your gray matter devoured.

Planning your escape route:

 Avoid any mazes, even if you are really good at finding your way out of mazes. You are escaping from zombies, not showing everyone how good you are at finding your way through a maze.

 Avoid main roads. Main roads will probably be blocked with cars, many of which will have zombie drivers. People who are stuck in traffic jams are very angry at the best of times, so imagine how angry a traffic jam of zombie drivers will be.

 You want to escape quickly, so avoid running through places that will slow you down—like a big sticky field of honey, or a mousetrap factory.

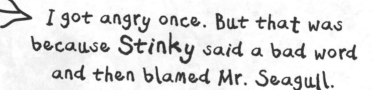

I got angry once. But that was because Stinky said a bad word and then blamed Mr. Seagull.

You should also take some essential items (like food and water) with you. The following is a list of things that you should avoid taking:

 Iron shoes—do not wear or carry heavy shoes made out of iron. Even if it means you have to escape wearing those flip flops you wear around the house or at the beach, iron footwear should be avoided at all costs.

 Anything else made of iron—in short, your Government suggests that escaping with objects made of iron is a big no-no. Iron is heavy. Therefore, do not take any of the following items when you flee (no matter how tempting):

- Iron hats
- Iron plates
- Iron owls, no matter how charming they are
- Iron shirts
- Four irons—this is no time for golf
- Ironing boards
- Iron irons—your clothes will be creased during the zombie apocalypse. Get used to it.

Zombie Apocalypse Dos and Don'ts

The following is a list of some very important DOS and DON'TS to ensure your safety during the zombie apocalypse.

DO

Protect your water supply at all costs. There's nothing worse than not being able to have a glass of water because a zombie has stuck his finger in the tap.

A zombie eating your brains is also pretty bad. I'd rather be thirsty and still have my brains than not thirsty and brain-free.

DON'T

Go into the cellar to investigate strange noises. Nothing good ever comes of this, trust us.

DO

Find someone heroic and handsome to be friends with. Handsome heroes always survive a zombie apocalypse. Perhaps you can fill the role of "lovable but goofy sidekick" and survive with them?

DON'T

Fall over. Clumsy people have no place in the zombie apocalypse. They always get their brains eaten first. Don't be that person

DO

Avoid graveyards. Graveyards are full of the undead, and they could pop up out of the ground at any moment to eat your brains. They're basically waiting rooms for zombies.

DON'T

Make loud noises. Singing will attract zombies, as they will think it's an invitation to a "brains party"—*your brains*. Also try to avoid yelping when you stub your toe, or laughing when you see something hilarious. Not that you will ever see such a thing ever again; the zombie apocalypse is no laughing matter.

Have My Brains Been Eaten? A Handy Checklist

Sometimes it isn't obvious if your brains have been eaten or not. One minute you can be happily walking down the street, and the next thing you know you've been attacked by a horde of ravenous zombies who have eaten your brains.

Therefore, it is advisable to stay cautious and watch out for any of the following signs of zombiefication:

Light-headedness

When your brains are eaten by a zombie, you will feel very light-headed. This is because you have no brains and your head is a lot lighter.

Happy zombies

If you see happy zombies (perhaps they are rubbing their tummies and smiling), they have probably just eaten some brains. Have they just eaten your brains? (see above).

Hating cheese sandwiches

Make a delicious cheese sandwich. Do you want to eat it? If you don't, and would prefer some delicious fresh brains instead, then you're a zombie. Sorry about that.

I got some new pants for my birthday.

Being green

Look in a mirror. Are you green? The undead are often green in color, so if you appear green there is a strong chance you are a zombie. Or a frog.

Bits falling off you

The undead suffer from what our scientists call "Parts Falling Off Syndrome." In layman's terms this means that parts of your body fall off, often at inappropriate times. Check your limbs. Have your fingers fallen off? Do you have both of your knees? And a head? If you don't, you're probably a zombie.

4. AFTERWARD

There is no afterward.

Well OK, I guess this is good-bye then?

Good-bye from Crazy Dave!

Got zombies? Get gardening!

The
Bloom & Doom
Seed Co.

Providing for all your apocalyptic gardening needs since 1968

"They're coming to get you, Barbara!"
—The sadly deceased brother of Bloom & Doom Seed founder Barbara Johns.